First published in France by Éditions Auzou, 2009
Original title: La Terre s'est enrhumée
© Éditions Philippe Auzou, Paris - France, 2009

Published in the United States and its territories by
HAMMOND WORLD ATLAS CORPORATION
Part of the Langenscheidt Publishing Group
36-36 33rd Street
Long Island City, NY 11106

Translator: Susan Allen Maurin

Printed and bound in China

ISBN-13: 978-0841-671409

The Earth Has Caught a Cold

Roxane Marie Galliez

Illustrated by Sandrine Lhomme

HAMMOND

The Earth has caught a cold.
This morning, I heard it coughing.
Its coughing fit made the ground shake.
Light tremors, like
An earthquake.

The Earth has caught a cold.
It's beginning to get a fever,
Its head is already so hot
The temperature of the sea has risen
by several degrees...

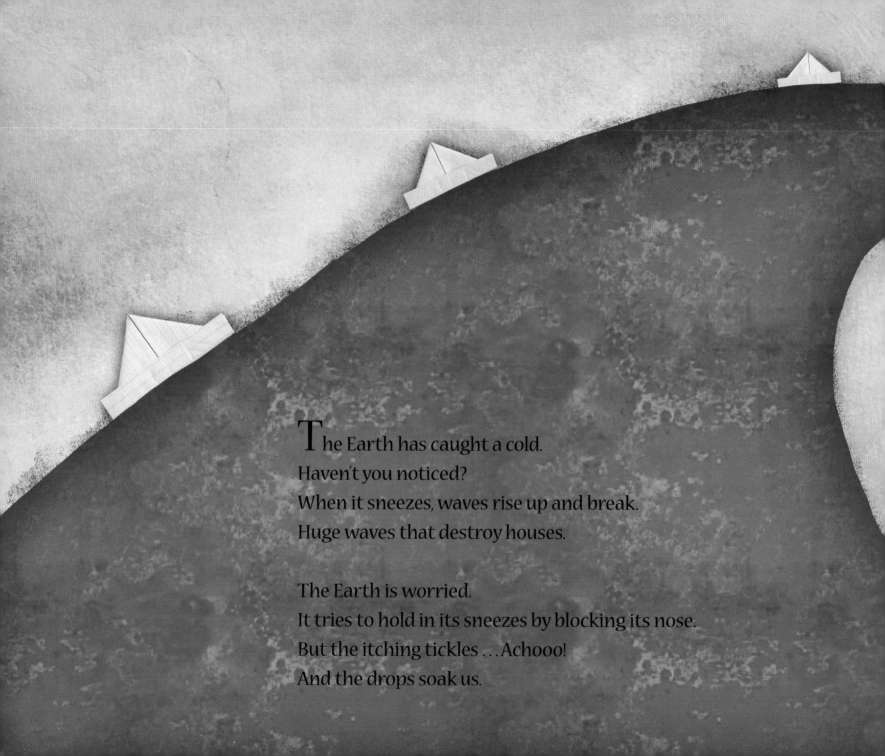

The Earth has caught a cold.
Haven't you noticed?
When it sneezes, waves rise up and break.
Huge waves that destroy houses.

The Earth is worried.
It tries to hold in its sneezes by blocking its nose.
But the itching tickles ... Achooo!
And the drops soak us.

The Earth is really sick, maybe from the flu.
Maybe it's just a sore throat.
Its throat burns, and outside it keeps getting warmer.
It wouldn't be surprising if lava started to erupt.

Someone has to say it: mankind has gone too far.
Pollution is never good.
All this black smoke makes the Earth very sad.
It can no longer breathe.

Use less water, make sure you close the taps,
Don't take everything that the Earth has to offer.
Let the Earth rest.

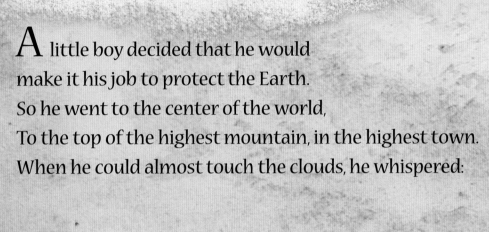

A little boy decided that he would
make it his job to protect the Earth.
So he went to the center of the world,
To the top of the highest mountain, in the highest town.
When he could almost touch the clouds, he whispered:

Then, the clouds stopped trembling.
Then, the birds stopped singing.
Then, the planes stopped flying.
Then, the factories stopped producing.
Then, the cars stopped driving.

Then, the men, women, and children listened . . .

"Shhhhhhhhhh!

SHHHHHHHH!"

They heard a heart beating slowly, and sniffling.

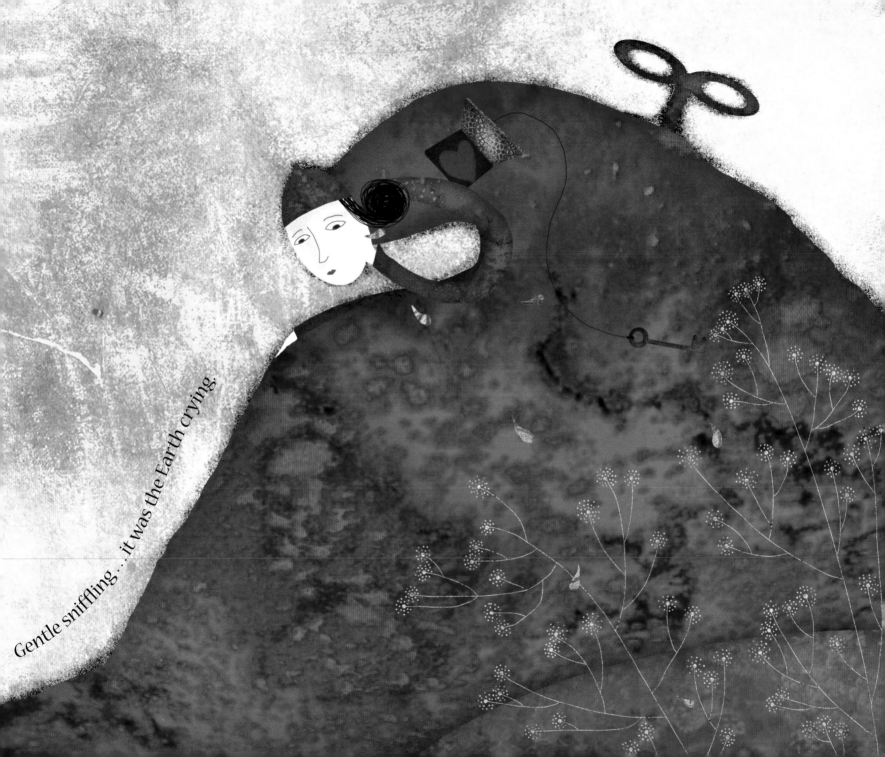

Gentle sniffling... it was the Earth crying.

So the men lay on the ground to comfort it,
And the women held hands to lull it to sleep.
And children picked up all the pieces of paper that were flying around.

Without making any noise, no noise at all ...

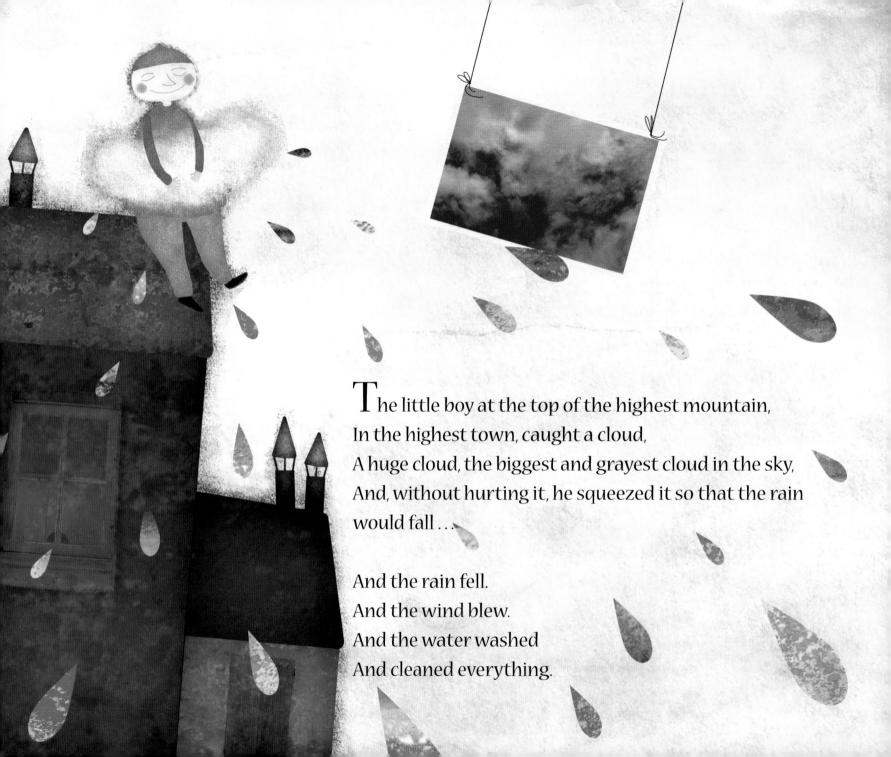

The little boy at the top of the highest mountain,
In the highest town, caught a cloud,
A huge cloud, the biggest and grayest cloud in the sky,
And, without hurting it, he squeezed it so that the rain
would fall …

And the rain fell.
And the wind blew.
And the water washed
And cleaned everything.

It was a wonderful moment,
Because the sun shone,
And a rainbow painted itself across the sky …

It's never too late to start all over again.